Jeoffry's Christmas

MARY BRYANT BAILEY

PICTURES BY ELIZABETH SAYLES

FARRAR STRAUS GIROUX • NEW YORK

Library of Congress Cataloging-in-Publication Data
Bailey, Mary Bryant.
    Jeoffry's Christmas / Mary Bryant Bailey ; pictures by Elizabeth Sayles.
        p.   cm.
    Summary: A kind cat helps a farmer find the right Christmas tree and assists Santa Claus in
delivering a Christmas feast to many animals.
    ISBN 0-374-33676-8
    [1. Cats—Fiction.   2. Christmas—Fiction.   3. Christmas trees—Fiction.   4. Santa Claus—
Fiction.   5. Animals—Fiction.   6. Stories in rhyme—Fiction.]   I. Sayles, Elizabeth, ill.   II. Title.

PZ8.3.B153 Je 2002
[E]—dc21

                                                                            2001046013

For Lucie and Willie

—*MBB*

For Matt and Jessica,

who melt the snow for me

—*ES*

The sun is shining on the snow.
We crunch across the bent meadow,
the farmer, his old dog, and me,
to find the perfect Christmas tree.
The farmer calls to me, "Jeoffry, kit!
Come here where it's warm, and sit."
The trembling dog, a nudge of my nose,
and up upon the seat he goes.

Off we fly in the horse-pulled sleigh,
and in the woods we'll spend the day.

Follow, follow
three chickadees,
me and the hound
around the trees.
We'll find the tree
that is so tall
it bumps the stars
and makes them fall.

I like a trunk
that I can sink
my claws into,
so I can slink
and sidle up
the bundled boughs
to greet the dove
with fond meows.

There, there it is!
Think tinsel and lights,
balls and baubles
gleaming at night!
There in shadow,
the perfect tree
that grows the blue
and green of sea.

A gang of caroling crows
passing by in scarves of snow
calls for me to come and play,
chase the farmer's horse-pulled sleigh.
I run until the orange light
becomes the silver rise of night.

I've wandered far, and I'm alone,
listening to the wild wind moan.
I hear the thrum and thump from here
of grouse wings and the hooves of deer.

A velvet snout pops through the snow,
not knowing which way to go.
There must be something I can do
to help a lost and hungry shrew.
And while I think, I'll take a rest.
This sack should make a cozy nest.

Waking to a whooshing sound,
Hey! I'm way above the ground,
high in Santa Claus's sleigh,
as he navigates the way.

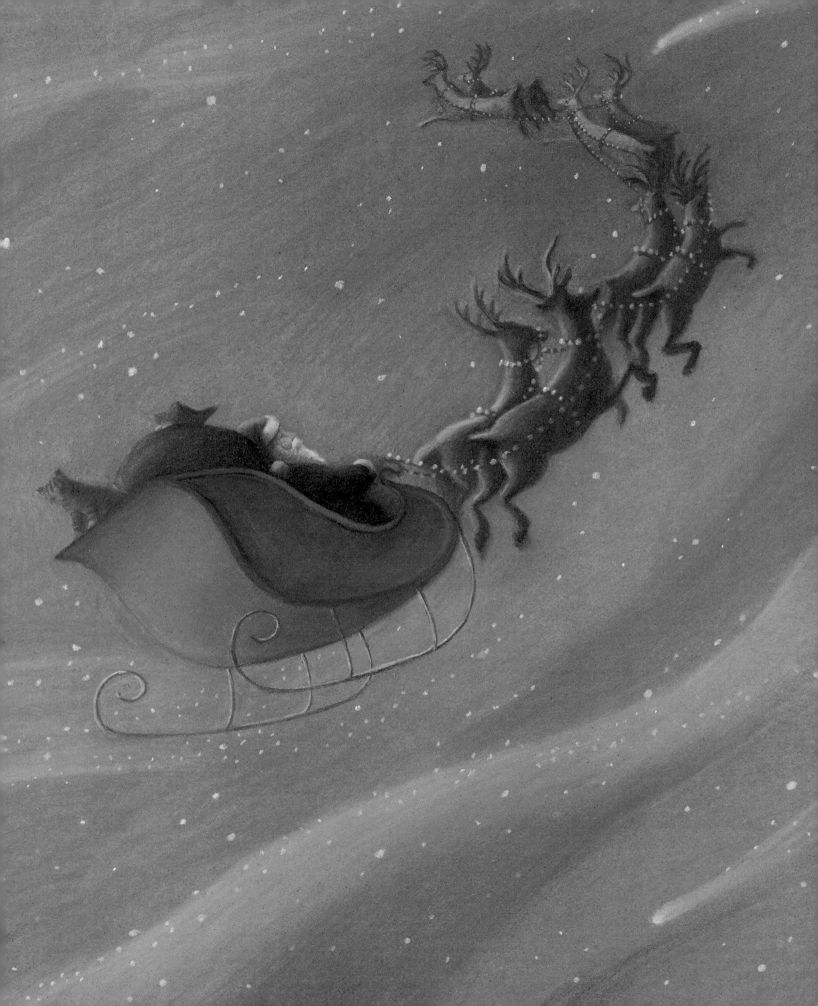

Passing by Cygnus the Swan,

Lepus the Hare, Orion,

Santa turns, says with a wink,

"I know why you're here, I think.

How'd you like to lend a hand,

scatter gifts across the land,

so each bird and every beast

will have a big Christmas feast?"

For rabbits, dandelion stew.

Poached salamanders for the shrew.

For skunks, a succotash of beets,

for deer and squirrel, shelled acorn meats.

Oak leaves for the white-footed mouse.

For little brown bats, stir-fried louse.

Grubs au gratin for tiller mole,

for muskrats, mussel casserole.

For the possum, persimmon bits,

for the raccoons, hominy grits.

For swans and geese, imported grains.

For the seagulls and for the cranes,

on the half shell cherrystone clams.

Rye grasses for the baby lambs.

For horses, balls of candied oat.

What's left over, for the goat.

It is nearly Christmas dawn.
Santa pats me with a yawn.
"For a friend you made a Christmas wish,
for you, a tin of nestled fish."

The sleigh slips down the drifted hills.
The farm a muffled silence fills.
Through the glass the shining tree!
The farmer pours some milk for me.

I curl up on the rug to rest.
At last I do what cats do best.